The Three Little

SUPERPIGS

AND THE GREAT EASTER EGG HUNT

For Joe, Amy, and Max. X

In loving memory of my wonderful Nan and Grandad. X

All rights reserved. Published by Scholastic Press, an imprint of Scholastic Inc.,
Publishers since 1920. SCHOLASTIC, SCHOLASTIC PRESS, and associated logos
are trademarks and/or registered trademarks of Scholastic Inc.

The publisher does not have any control over and does not assume any
responsibility for author or third-party websites or their content.

This book is a work of fiction. Names, characters, places, and incidents are either the
product of the author's imagination or are used fictitiously, and any resemblance to actual persons,
living or dead, business establishments, events, or locales is entirely coincidental.

Library of Congress Cataloging-in-Publication Data available

ISBN 978-1-338-87584-3

10 9 8 7 6 5 4 3 2 1   24 25 26 27 28

Printed in the U.S.A.   76

First edition, January 2024

The text type was set in Mrs Ant Regular. The display type was set in YWFT Merry Filled.

The Three Little
SUPERPIGS

AND THE GREAT EASTER EGG HUNT

Written and Illustrated by

Claire Evans

Scholastic Press
New York

It was springtime in Fairyland.
The whole town was having fun
at the annual Easter Egg Hunt.

The Three Little SUPERPIGS loved Easter eggs
and wanted to find as many as possible.

Once their baskets were piled high, the SUPERPIGS began devouring their delicious candy.

The first SUPERPIG ate his candy in size order, starting with the biggest.

The second SUPERPIG ate his treats with a spoon, scooping out all the candy from the middle.

The third SUPERPIG cracked open all his eggs and savored his candy one piece at a time.

After they had finished all their candy,
the pigs wanted . . .

"MORE! . . ."

"MORE! . . ."

"MORE!"

They hunted all over,
but the greedy little pigs
just couldn't find
any more.

As they slumped back home,
they ran into a boy named Jack.

He told them of a magical city in the sky,
where a magic goose laid the biggest, shiniest,
most extraordinary, golden chocolate eggs.

Jack handed the SUPERPIGS some magic beans.
"These beans will grow into an enormous beanstalk
and will lead you up to the AMAZING eggs," he explained.

But he warned that the magic goose who lays these eggs
was being held captive by a ghastly GIANT.

"We're not scared of a GIANT!" said the SUPERPIGS
as they raced back home to plant the magic beans.
They covered them carefully with soil, watered them, then waited...

and waited...   and waited.

And the
next morning…

WHOOSH!!

An enormous beanstalk shot up into the sky!

Thrilled by the thought of more eggs, the SUPERPIGS grabbed their empty Easter baskets and clambered up the giant plant.

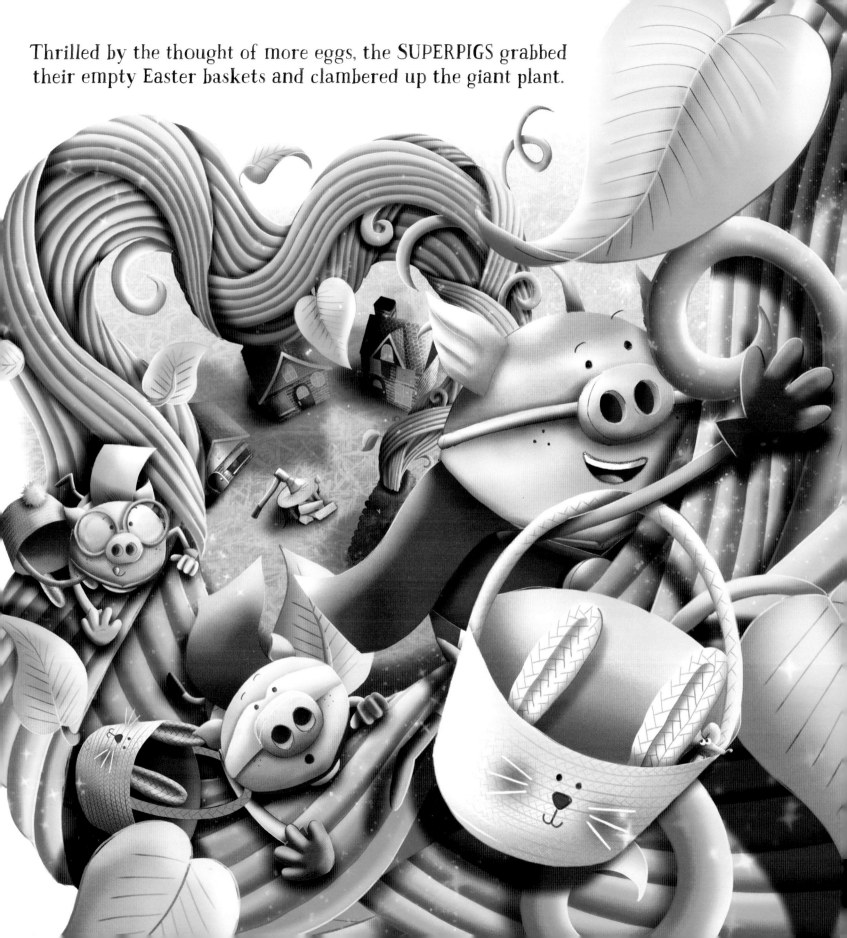

At the top of the beanstalk, the SUPERPIGS gasped
in amazement at the City in the Sky. They were surrounded by
the most glorious golden eggs they had EVER seen!
"Wow! Jack was right!" the SUPERPIGS exclaimed.

The excited pigs got to work, greedily filling
their baskets with as many chocolate eggs as possible . . .

. . . until they spotted
the magic goose
who was tied up,
looking very sad
and in need of help.

The SUPERPIGS
realized they had
been too focused
on collecting eggs
for themselves
and decided to
help set the poor
goose free.

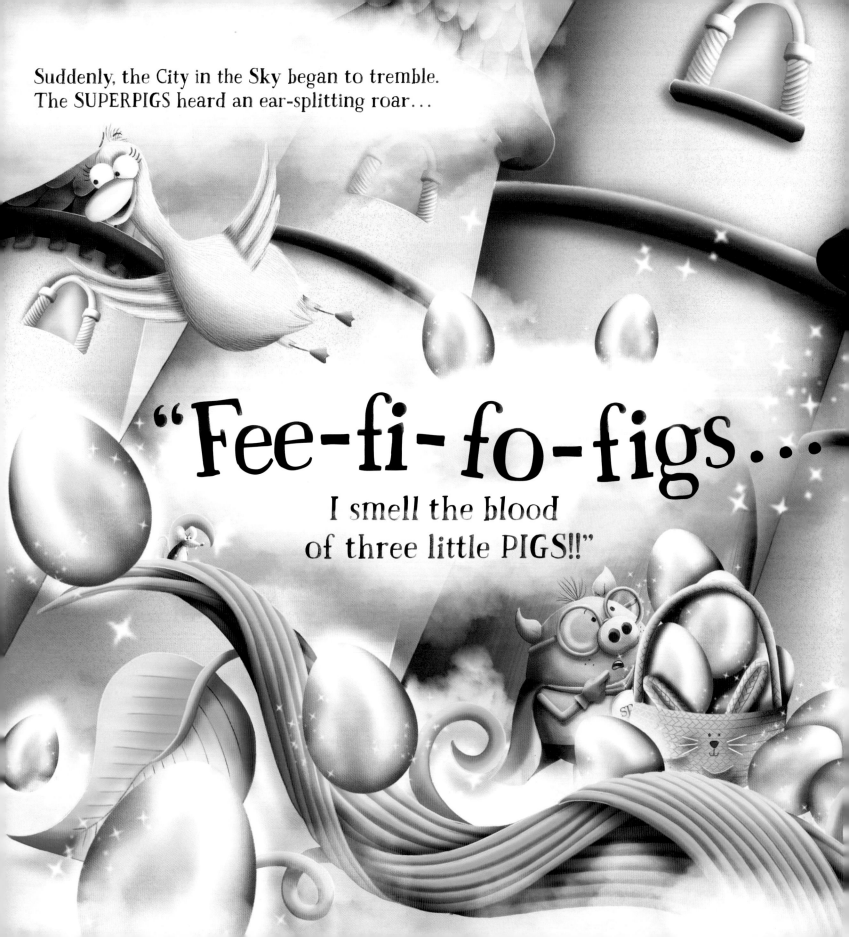

Suddenly, the City in the Sky began to tremble.
The SUPERPIGS heard an ear-splitting roar...

"Fee-fi-fo-figs...

I smell the blood
of three little PIGS!!"

"That sounds like the BIG BAD WOLF!" gasped the SUPERPIGS.

But it wasn't the BIG BAD WOLF...

"He he he! What a delightful treat:
Three juicy Easter hams to EAT!"

"We don't think so!" the SUPERPIGS cried,
and they leapt out of the Giant Bad Wolf's grasp.

They fled from the beast as fast as they could,
heading back toward the beanstalk.
The **Giant Bad Wolf** was gaining on them,
but the SUPERPIGS had a plan.

Sacrificing their new golden eggs,
they emptied their baskets
behind them.

THUD!

The giant villain hurtled into the air
and crash-landed onto his back.

The first SUPERPIG
used his empty basket
to hold the Wolf down.

Then the
second SUPERPIG
tied him up with vines.

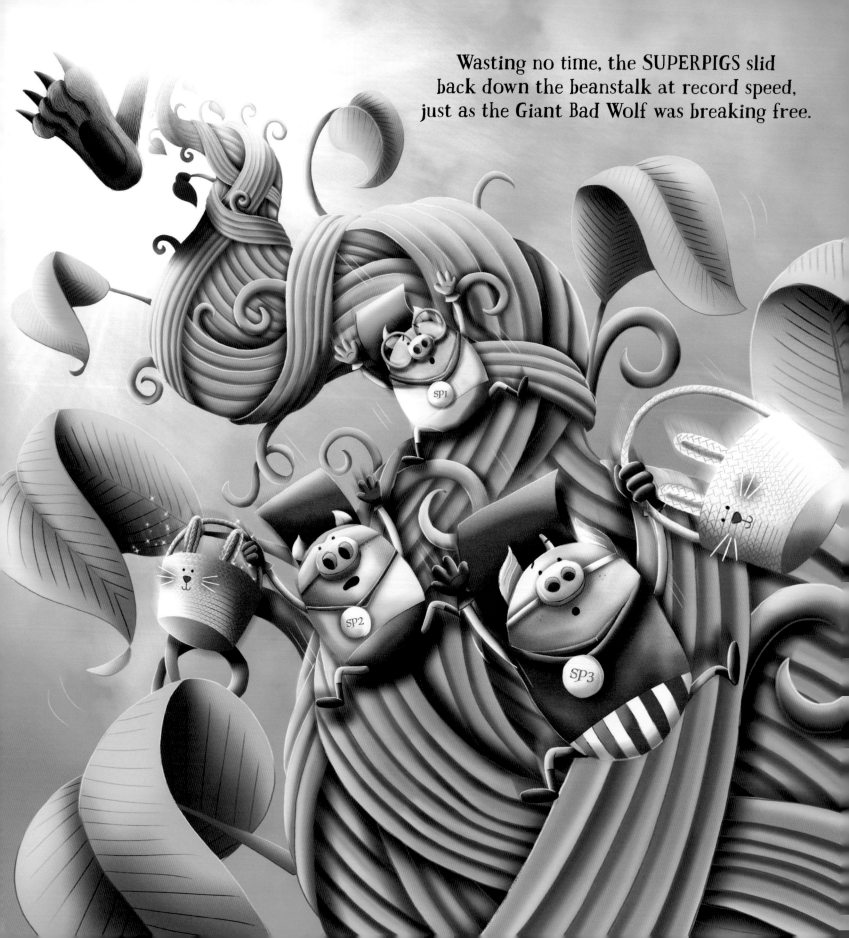

Wasting no time, the SUPERPIGS slid
back down the beanstalk at record speed,
just as the Giant Bad Wolf was breaking free.

When they reached the bottom, the third SUPERPIG
grabbed a nearby axe and began chopping
at the gigantic plant.

THWACK!

THWACK!

THWACK!

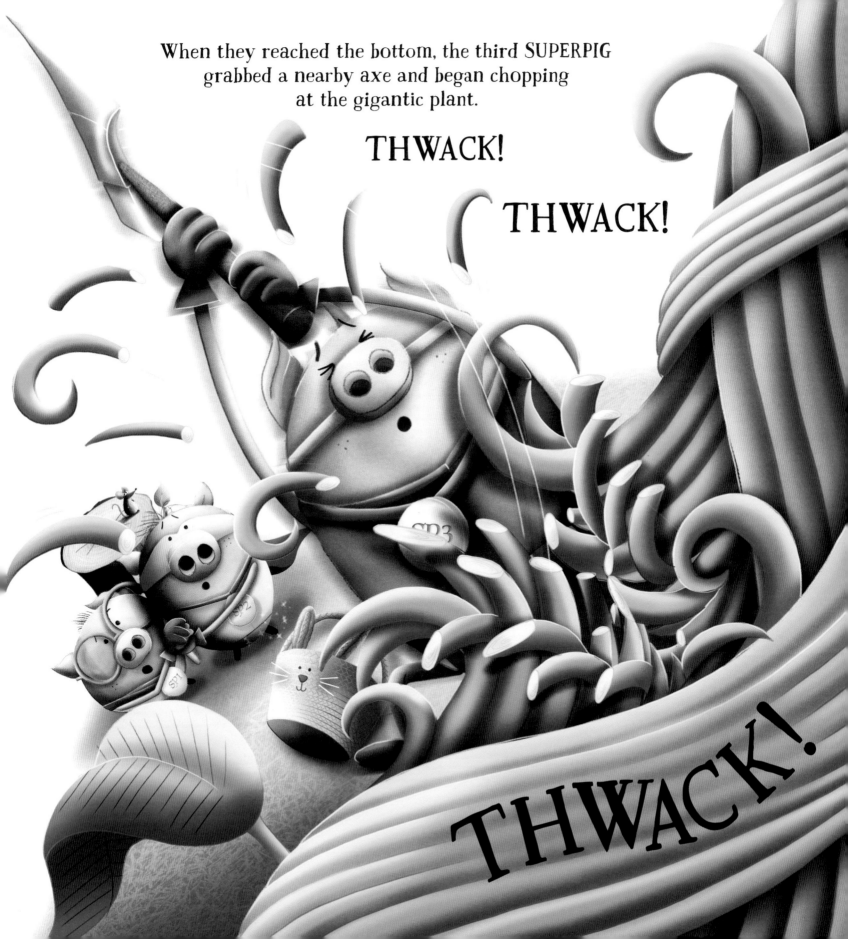

With one final blow, the enormous beanstalk fell to the ground.

CRASH!

The Giant Bad Wolf was now trapped in the sky and Fairyland was safe once more.

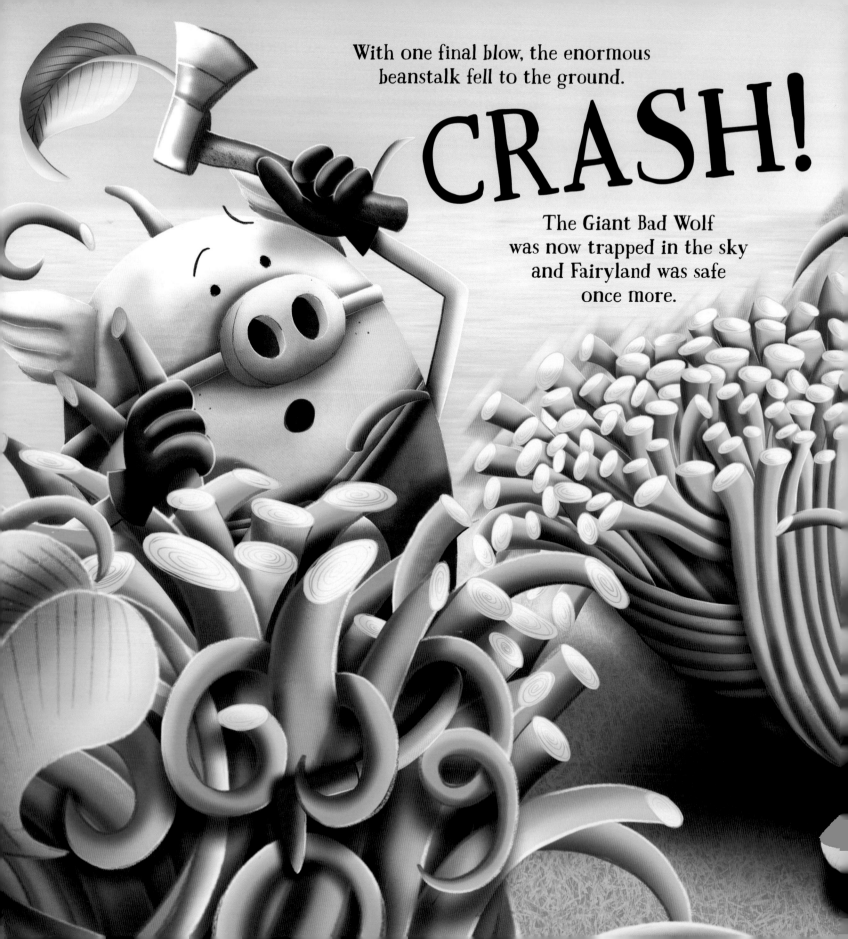

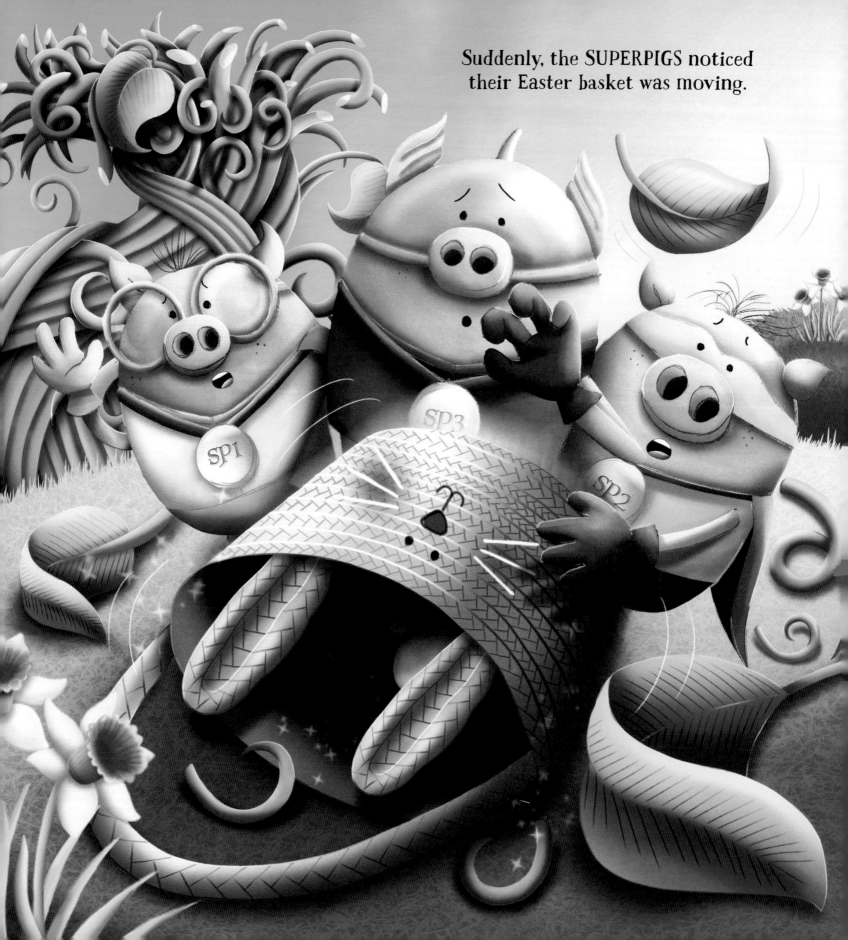

Suddenly, the SUPERPIGS noticed
their Easter basket was moving.

"The magic goose!"
laughed the SUPERPIGS.

The goose thanked them
for saving her from the **Giant Bad Wolf**
and offered them her
golden eggs as a reward.

The pigs were thrilled but had learned
their lesson not to be too greedy...

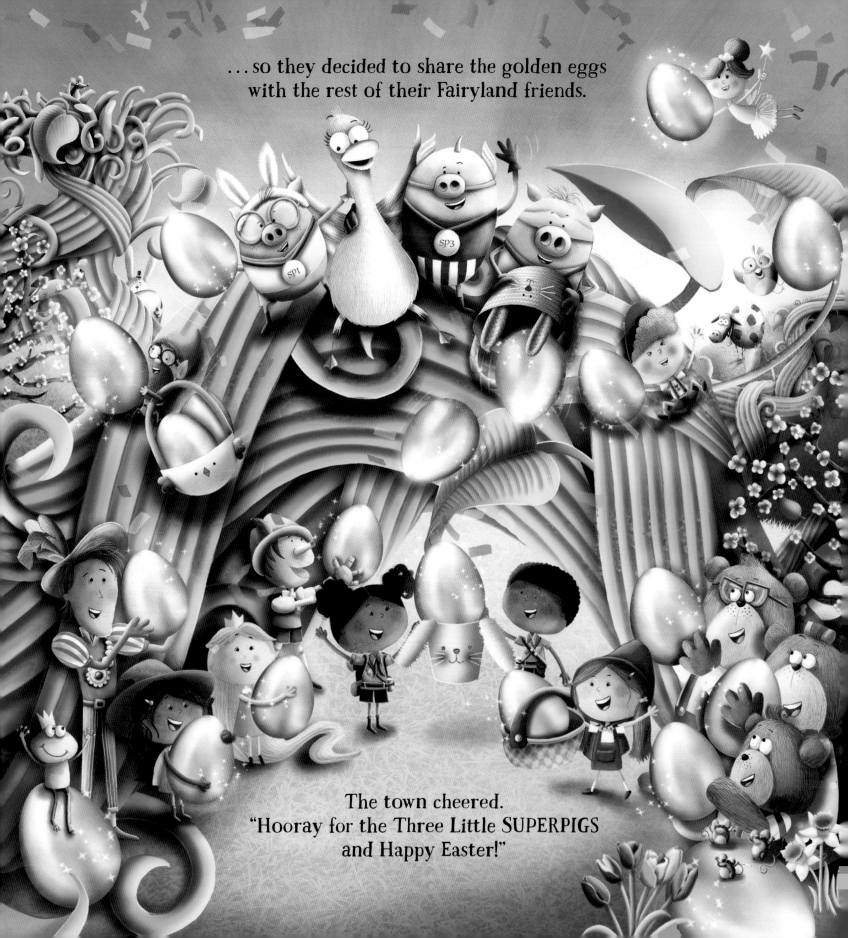

...so they decided to share the golden eggs with the rest of their Fairyland friends.

The town cheered.
"Hooray for the Three Little SUPERPIGS and Happy Easter!"

The End?

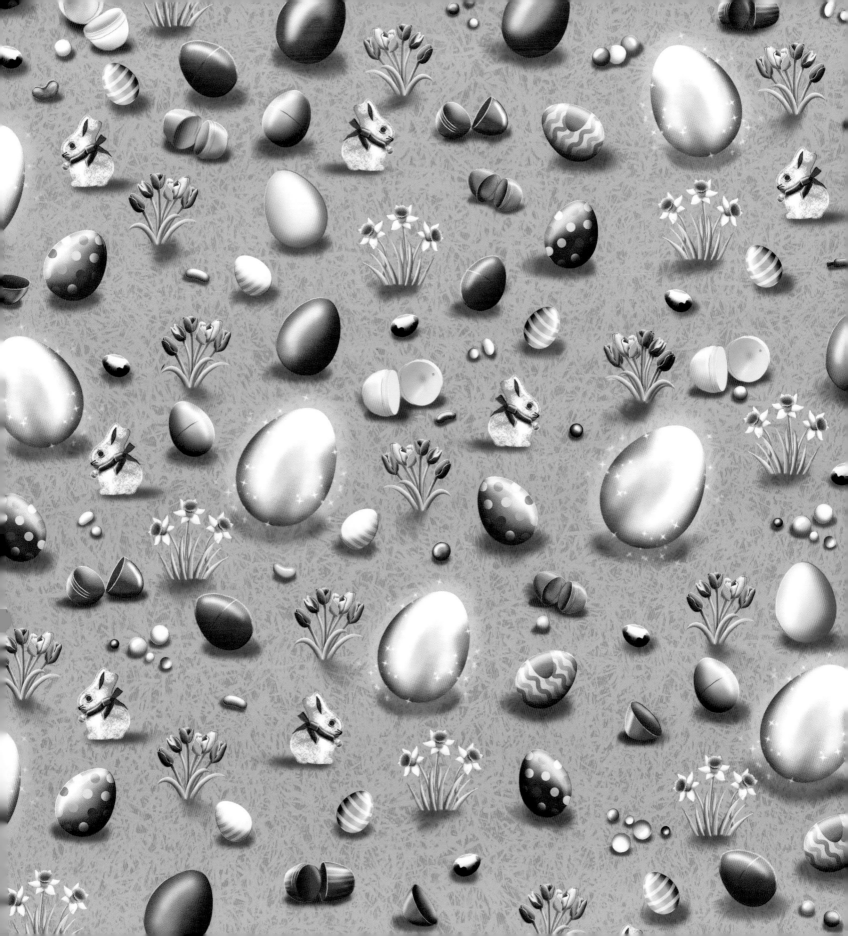